# When the City Sleeps

SHANI DENISE

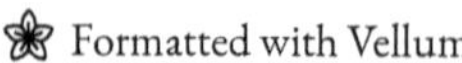 Formatted with Vellum

# About the Author

Shani Denise
writes soulful, spicy urban romances that explore Black Love
in all its beauty, and magic. A Detroit native, she brings the
city's grit and warmth to every page.
This book is dedicated to those who I've had the pleasure to
call mom, dad and nana. They are a collective of individuals
who have always pushed me, believed in me and even though
some have passed on and are no longer with me, they will
always be represented in anything that I do!
I love you Forever.

# Acknowledgments

This story was created with so much love, and I couldn't have done it without the incredible support, encouragement, and guidance I've received along the way. I am deeply and eternally grateful to every single person who helped bring this project to life.

A heartfelt thank you to my husband for being my constant source of support, to my baby brother for reading my work and sharing his insights, and to my cousin Tahitia for always pushing me toward greatness. To my amazing ARC team, to Tasha for both merch and beta reading, and to Monet for bringing her creative touch to the graphics—I appreciate you more than words can express.

I also want to thank The Morning Collective for the fun, insightful conversations about the spicy scenes and for their encouragement throughout the process. And finally, a special thank you to Danielle Thomas for her beautiful poetic contribution in chapter five.

This book would not be the same without all of you.

# ONE

# The First Collision

The city never really slept. Even when the clock slid past midnight and the rest of the world tucked itself into silence, Detroit kept humming like it was wired to an endless beat. The streetlights buzzed faintly, neon signs flickered over corner stores, and the low thrum of bass rattled out of passing cars. Even the air carried a rhythm—thick, heavy with August humidity, laced with fried food grease, gas fumes, and the faint sweetness of night-blooming flowers from somebody's neglected garden down the block.

Nia Carter hugged her denim jacket tighter across her chest as she stepped out of the lounge where she'd been waitressing since June. The Jefferson Avenue strip looked almost deserted at first glance, but she knew better. The city never gave you everything at once. You had to pay attention.

She shifted her bag higher on her shoulder, while taking in her surroundings the way her mama had taught her years ago. *Never let them catch you off guard, baby girl. Keep your eyes sharp, your head up, and your steps quick.*

Nia lived by that advice, though some nights—like tonight—it felt heavier than others.

Her feet ached from standing for eight hours straight, her

curls had frizzed from the steam of the kitchen, and her tip money weighed light in her purse. Still, she refused to let the exhaustion show. Not to the men who leaned against corner walls with their sly stares. Not to the car that slowed at the red light, headlights dragging over her body like hands. Not even to herself.

She walked fast, long strides, chin high. The cracked sidewalk forced her to watch her footing, but her eyes scanned every reflection in darkened windows. She was almost at the corner when she heard it—the low purr of an engine creeping too slow.

Her pulse jumped.

A black Dodge Charger rolled into view, glossy as midnight, the deep hum of its motor vibrating against her chest.

She froze for a half-second before picking up her pace, telling herself not to look. Nia just kept walking.

The car matched her rhythm, not too close, not too far. Just enough to make her nerves jump.

Then the tinted window slid down.

"Yo," a voice called, low and smooth.

Nia's grip tightened on her bag strap. She turned her head, ready to sharpen her tongue at whoever thought they could roll up on her at midnight. But the words stalled on her lips.

The man in the driver's seat wasn't what she expected.

Instead of some old head trying to spit tired game, her eyes locked on a younger man—late twenties, maybe early thirties, brown moisturized skin—hazel eyes catching the glares from the streetlights like glass. Tattoos ran along his forearm, dark ink fading slightly with time, and a diamond stud in his ear that winked at her. His fitted cap shaded his sharp jawline, but nothing could dim the quiet authority in his posture.

He was handsome, but not in the polished, safe kind of way. No, this man looked like trouble. The kind of trouble that made you lean closer, even when your better judgment screamed no and to run.

"You dropped this." His voice carried that drawl, the kind that made words roll slow, deliberate.

Nia blinked. "What?"

He held up a phone. Her phone. Her cracked iPhone 11, the one she hadn't even realized slid from her jacket pocket.

"Oh, damn." Relief washed through her chest, then embarrassment came just as quickly. She stepped toward the car cautiously. "Thanks."

He leaned across the seat, extending the phone through the open window. He smelled expensive, and like a grown man. When their fingers brushed—just for a second—something electric surged up her arm. Static, like the kind that prickled you when you brushed against someone in winter. Electric. The touch was electric.

She pulled her hand back too fast, shoving the phone into her bag, pretending like she hadn't felt it.

"You good?" His gaze lingered, steady, unreadable.

"I'm fine," she said quickly, maybe too quickly.

He tilted his head, studying her like he didn't quite believe it. Then, with the ghost of a smile tugging at his lips, he added, "You shouldn't be out here walking with your head down. City don't play nice."

Nia straightened her shoulders. "I can handle myself."

His chuckle was low, teasing. "I bet you can. But still... it wouldn't hurt to let somebody look out for you. Let me give you a ride."

Her eyes narrowed. "Do I look like the type to hop in cars with strangers?"

He smirked, unfazed. "Depends on the stranger."

There it was again—that steady look, like he was seeing straight through the layers she kept tucked away from everybody else. And Nia hated how her pulse betrayed her, skipping like it had a mind of its own.

She lifted her chin. "I'm good on the ride. Thanks, though."

He held up a hand, no pressure in his voice. "Respect. I get it. Name's D. I mean Darius"

She hesitated. Common sense told her to keep walking, to let this be a moment that slipped away like so many others. But curiosity got the best of her. "Nia."

His smirk softened into something that almost looked like approval. "Nia. Pretty name. Matches the vibe."

Her stomach fluttered, heat creeping up her neck. She forced a shrug, trying not to let it show. "Goodnight, D, I mean Darius."

She turned, heading toward the corner. She could feel his eyes on her, heavy as the streetlights.

"Guess I'll see you around, Nia," he called out, that lazy confidence dripping from every word. "City too small not to."

She didn't reply. She didn't look back. But when she caught her reflection in a store window a block later, she saw it: the small, unshakable curve of her lips. A smile she hadn't given permission to exist.

And just like that, D had lodged himself into her night—and maybe, against her better judgment, into something more.

TWO

# Temptation in the Air

The morning sun hit the city with a reluctant glare, spilling gold across cracked sidewalks and graffiti-splashed walls. Detroit's streets smelled of hot asphalt, coffee from corner cafes, and the faint tang of exhaust fumes.

Nia walked fast, earbuds in, pretending she wasn't still thinking about Darius. Why did he have to have those eyes? She scolded herself internally, tugging at the strap of her bag. *You barely know him. But why can't I stop thinking about him?*

But the memory of their first encounter lingered—his smirk, the slow drawl of his voice, the way his fingers brushed hers. She shook her head and focused on her steps, telling herself she had more important things to worry about. Like the mountain of deliveries, she needed to make for her catering side hustle before her first grad school class tonight.

She turned the corner onto Jefferson again, and the street was alive in the kind of way that made her pulse pick up: the hum of early traffic, kids on skateboards, a man selling cold drinks out of a cooler on the sidewalk, and the faint echo of a saxophone from a corner porch.

Then she heard it, a familiar growl of an engine. Her chest tightened involuntarily.

The black Dodge Charger rolled into view, slow, deliberate. D.

Nia wanted to turn and walk faster, but curiosity won over. D caught her glance and waved with one hand, casual, like they'd been friends for years.

She tried to look unimpressed. "What are you doing up this early?" she called out, a little louder than intended.

He leaned against the hood, arms crossed, sunlight glinting off the diamond in his ear. "Business never sleeps," he said with a grin. "And apparently, neither do you."

Nia rolled her eyes but couldn't stop the grin creeping onto her face. "I have stuff to do."

"Stuff can wait," he countered smoothly. "Come chill. Ten minutes. I'll make it worth your time."

She laughed, a short, incredulous sound. "What? Are you going to bribe me with coffee now?"

"Maybe," he said, his grin widening. "Or maybe I'm just here to remind you that walking alone in the city isn't as safe as you think."

She huffed, pretending to scowl, but she stepped closer, her curiosity stronger than her caution. "You're intense."

"Depends who you ask," he said, eyes glinting. "Some people call it confidence. Others... trouble."

That word made her pulse jump. Trouble. Dangerous. Yet, something in his gaze dared her to lean in, to see past the carefully built walls she wore every day.

They walked together toward a nearby café, the streets waking around them, windows catching the gold of sunrise. Nia felt herself relax slightly, despite the tension curling in her stomach.

"So," D said, tilting his head as they approached the entrance, "you been here before?"

Nia laughed. "Funny. You think I'm the type to come to cafés at sunrise?"

"You're full of surprises," he said, sliding the door open for her. "And I like that."

Inside, the café smelled of roasted coffee beans and pastries. The barista gave them a nod, clearly familiar with D. He waved, and she noticed—he had presence, a way of moving through space that made heads turn without him even trying.

They ordered drinks, and while D teased her about her choice of caramel latte, Nia found herself laughing more freely than she had in weeks. Something about his energy was infectious, the way he spoke like the city was his playground and he wanted to share it with her.

They took a small table near the window, the sun spilling over their hands as they both sipped their drinks. D leaned in slightly, just enough that she caught the faint scent of his cologne—warm, spicy, a little like cedar and something she couldn't place.

"You know," he said, voice low, "you got that look like you're ready to take on the world... but the world hasn't seen it yet."

Nia tilted her head, surprised by his observation. "Is that supposed to be a compliment or a warning?"

He smiled, that slow, teasing smirk. "Both. Depends on how you take it."

The air between them thickened, tension curling like smoke. Nia tried to focus on her latte, but her eyes kept flicking back to him, the way his jaw flexed when he spoke, the casual confidence in his posture, the intensity in his gaze.

D reached across the table, just brushing his hand against hers. Nia froze, nerves buzzing through her. She pulled her hand back slightly, heart racing, but he didn't push it further —just let his fingers linger close enough that the warmth still hummed in her skin.

"You're dangerous," she murmured, half to herself.

"And yet," he said, leaning back just enough to smirk, "here you are. Talking to me anyway."

Their laughter blended with the city sounds outside—the honk of horns, the distant wail of a train, the clatter of a delivery truck down the street. Everything felt electric, like the city itself was conspiring to pull them closer together.

Nia couldn't deny it. The pull between them was magnetic, a current she couldn't fight even if she tried. She glanced at him, then down at her latte, then back again.

D's gaze held hers, unwavering. "I don't do small talk," he said quietly. "If we're gonna be around each other... might as well be real."

On the inside, Nia felt a flutter, part fear, part thrill. The city streets, the café, the morning light—they all seemed suspended, waiting for her decision.

Smirking, she replied. "Who said we're going to be around each other?"

He just looked at her, a wry smile curling the edges of his lips.

And in that moment, she realized she wanted to find out where this would go.

THREE

# Secrets Between Us

The night came back heavy, thick with late-summer heat. Downtown pulsed with music spilling from bars and car stereos, but Nia sat on the edge of her apartment's fire escape, letting the city's hum settle into her bones.

She hugged her knees, staring down at the street below. Her building wasn't much—a faded brick three-story on the Eastside—but from her spot on the rusty black iron, she could see the skyline glowing in the distance, tall buildings blinking like they were winking secrets at her.

Her phone buzzed.

D.

She stared at the name, biting her lip. He'd texted her a couple of times since having coffee that morning—playful things, nothing too heavy—but she hadn't answered. She told herself she was busy with prep for her catering orders, but the truth was simpler: D rattled her.

And Nia didn't like being rattled.

The phone buzzed again.

D: You ignoring me or nah?

Nia smiled despite herself. She typed back, fingers hesitant at first.



His reply came fast.



Her brows shot up. She leaned over the edge of the fire escape—and there he was. Parked across the street, leaning against that black Charger like he owned the whole damn block. Arms crossed, head tilted up at her, smirk in place.

"Seriously?" she called down, trying not to laugh.

"Dead serious," he shouted back. "Come down."

Her neighbors were probably watching from their windows, and she hated giving people something to gossip about. But the thrill in her chest outweighed the hesitation. She climbed down carefully, her sandals clanking against the iron steps.

D's gaze followed her every move, steady, unflinching. When her feet hit the pavement, he shook his head with a grin. "Dangerous climbing down like that in a skirt."

"Then stop staring," she shot back, hands on her hips.

"Can't help it," he said simply.

The way he said it made her skin warm. He gestured toward the car. "Ride with me."

She hesitated, but the city around them felt alive tonight—like something might happen if she just stopped playing it safe. So, she slid into the passenger seat.

The Charger's leather smelled faintly of cologne and smoke, and the bass of the music vibrating from the speakers made her chest buzz. D drove smoothly, one hand on the wheel, the other resting loosely on his thigh. He didn't push conversation at first; he just let the city lights flicker across their faces as he cruised down Jefferson, then deeper into the heart of downtown.

Finally, he spoke. "So what's your story, Nia? Besides waitressing and avoiding rides from strangers."

She smirked faintly. "I'm in grad school. Well—trying to be. Classes start this fall. I'm hustling catering on the side, working at the lounge at night. Trying to find my footing, wherever that leads me."

"You want to leave the D?" he asked.

"Not forever," she said quickly. "This is home. But sometimes it feels like the city just... eats people alive. And I don't want that to be me."

He nodded slowly, his eyes thoughtful. "Respect. You got plans. Most people don't."

She tilted her head. "And what about you? You just ride around at midnight collecting lost phones?"

He chuckled, shaking his head. "Nah. That's just how I met you. I do... a little of everything. Got my hands in some businesses. Some of it clean. Some of it... not so much."

Nia studied him, trying to read between the lines. His voice carried no shame, no excuses. Just truth, raw and unpolished.

"So, you're telling me you're trouble, Big D, or should I call you Darius?

"Didn't I already warn you? And you can call me Darius; I like how you say it." he replied, flashing a grin.

But she caught the flicker behind his eyes, something heavier. A weight.

"What's the 'not so much' part mean?" she pressed.

He tightened his grip on the wheel. For a moment, the only sound was the hum of the engine and the city sliding past outside. Then he said quietly, "Let's just say I learned young that the city don't give you nothin' free. Sometimes you take opportunities where they come. Even if they ain't the kind you can put on a resume."

Nia let that sit between them. She'd seen enough in her own life to know what he meant without needing details.

"Everybody's got a story," she murmured.

D glanced at her, his eyes softer now. "Really? So, what's yours?"

She hesitated, her chest tightening. She thought about her father, the man who disappeared when she was twelve. About her mother, worn down from years of double shifts at the plant. About the weight she carried, always trying to be enough for them both.

But she didn't say all that. Not yet.

Instead, she said, "My story's still being written."

D nodded slowly, like he respected that answer. "Fair enough."

They pulled up to the riverfront, the Detroit River stretching wide under the night sky. The lights of Windsor twinkled across the water, close enough to touch but just out of reach. D parked, turned off the engine, and for a moment the silence pressed in, broken only by them getting out the car and hearing the water lapping against the rocks.

Nia leaned against the car, breathing in the night. D stood close—too close—and when she glanced up, his eyes were on her.

"You ever feel like the city only sleeps when it wants to?" he asked, voice low.

She smiled faintly. "All the time."

The air between them thickened, and for a heartbeat, she thought he might kiss her. Instead, he brushed his thumb along her jaw, so light it sent a shiver racing through her.

"Nia," he murmured, her name heavy with something unspoken.

Her breath caught. For the first time in a long time, she

felt like someone was really seeing her—not just the student, the worker, the girl hustling to keep her head above water. But the real her.

And that scared her more than anything.

# FOUR

# Giving In

The following weekend came wrapped in heavy heat, the kind that stuck to skin and made tempers flare in traffic. Nia had finished a catering order run and was heading back to her apartment when she saw the Charger again, black paint gleaming under the streetlights like it had been washed that morning.

D leaned against the hood, arms crossed, phone in hand. A couple of guys on the corner dapped him up, quick and respectful, before drifting away. Nia noticed how people seemed to move around him—careful, like he carried weight that demanded space.

But when his hazel eyes landed on her, the smirk softened.

"Hey, grad school," he called, pushing off the hood.

She rolled her eyes, but her lips betrayed her with the smallest smile. "Is that my name now?"

"Nah," he said, his voice dropping low as he stepped closer. "Your name's Nia. I just like reminding you I know what you're grinding for."

Her heart stuttered at the way he said her name, slow and deliberate, like he was tasting it.

"What are you doing here?" she asked, trying to keep her voice steady.

"Making sure you eat something besides coffee and air," he said, lifting a takeout bag. "Got us plates from Armandos."

She blinked. "You brought me food?"

"Don't sound so shocked." He chuckled. "Even Big D eats sometimes."

The way those words slid from his mouth reminded her of what people called him in the streets. But with her, he wasn't just D, or the King of the streets. He was Darius. The difference pressed heavily on her chest as he followed her up to her place.

Inside, her apartment was small but cozy—plants on the windowsill, books stacked on the table, the faint scent of vanilla from a candle she'd lit earlier. Darius set the bag down, glancing around with quiet interest.

"Nice spot," he said, loosening his cap. "Feels like you here. Soft, but strong."

Nia busied herself unpacking the food to hide the way her cheeks warmed. "Don't get poetic on me now."

He laughed low, the sound rumbling in her chest. "Not my fault you bring it outta me."

They sat at the table, eating straight out of the containers. Between bites, they talked—about music, about the city, about childhood memories. Nia found herself laughing, real laughter that bubbled up without force.

But as the night stretched, the air shifted. His hand brushed hers when he reached for a fork. His knee bumped her under the table and didn't move. Every glance he gave her lingered a second too long.

Finally, he pushed back his chair. "You mind if I step out to blow one?"

She followed him to the fire escape, the same iron she used to sit on alone at night. The city stretched out before them, glowing and restless, car horns echoing faintly in the distance.

Darius leaned against the railing lighting the blunt, he was close enough that she could feel his body heat. He didn't look at her at first, just at the skyline. "Out here, everybody thinks they know me, "D". The one who handles business. The one you don't cross. But with you..." He paused, blowing out the smoke, turning his gaze to her. "With you, I don't wanna be D."

Her breath caught. His honesty cracked something inside her, something she'd been holding tight.

"Then who do you wanna be?" she whispered.

His lips curved faintly. "Just Nia's Darius."

His words sat between them like a promise.

Nia didn't think. She stepped closer, her fingers brushing his arm. His gaze dropped to her mouth, and before she could second-guess it, he leaned in.

The first kiss was slow, searching. His lips were warm, firm, tasting faintly of weed from the blunt he'd been smoking. She melted into it, her hands sliding up to his chest. He deepened the kiss, one hand cupping her jaw, thumb stroking her cheek like she was something fragile and rare.

Her back pressed against the railing, his body crowding hers, but she didn't feel trapped. She felt claimed, in the softest, most dangerous way.

When he finally pulled back, his forehead rested against hers, their breaths mingling in the humid night air.

"Darius," she whispered, tasting his name like it was only meant for her.

He closed his eyes, a faint smile tugging at his lips. "Say it again."

She did. And with every repetition, she knew she was slipping deeper into something she couldn't pull away from.

Because D belonged to the streets.

But Darius... Darius was hers.

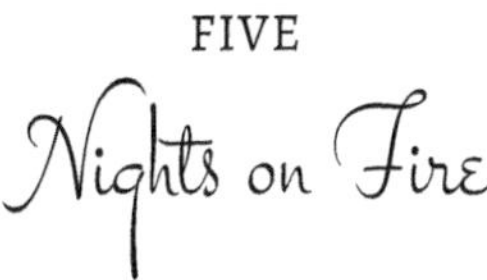

# FIVE

The week after their first kiss stretched out like a taut string, humming between them.

Every time Nia thought of Darius, her stomach flipped. His lips, the way he held her against his skin, the way the city seemed to pause when he touched her.

She tried to bury herself in work—classes, catering, shifts at the lounge—but Darius kept showing up. Sometimes with food, sometimes with just his car parked outside her building like a shadow she secretly looked forward to.

And every time, the tension grew sharper.

One Thursday night, after a particularly brutal shift at the lounge, she stepped outside expecting silence. Instead, the black Charger idled by the curb, headlights washing the sidewalk in pale glow.

Darius leaned against the driver's door, phone in hand. When he looked up, his smirk was immediate. "You always make people wait this long?"

Her lips curved despite her exhaustion. "You always stalk girls outside their jobs?"

He pushed off the car, strolling toward her with that slow,

deliberate gait that made her heart race. "Not girls," he said softly. "Just you."

Her breath hitched.

He opened the passenger door, waiting. Against her better judgment, Nia slid inside.

The city blurred past in streaks of neon and shadows as Darius drove. His hand rested on the gearshift, close enough to hers that the space between their fingers felt charged. She wanted to reach out, to bridge the gap, but the tension was its own kind of pleasure. Nia began to jot down a poem about the way he made her feel.

"I Never Tell You"
I could never tell you
how wet I get every time you speak.
Not when you're just talking,
but when your voice drops low & steady,
like you already own every part of me.
I could never tell you
how when we were in the car,
you focused on the road,
and I was sitting there,
clenching so hard,
my pussy begging for your hands, your mouth,
For you to slide inside me.
I could never tell you
that when you laugh,
I'm not just smiling
I'm imagining your tongue sliding down my neck,
your hands pulling my hair,
While you fuck me slow,
making me beg with every stroke .
I could never tell you
how many nights I've ridden you in my head
slow, deep, raw,
you feeling how tight and wet I am,

your voice low in my ear,
telling me exactly how you want it,
while I moan inside,
already shaking before you even touch me.
I could never tell you
that when I go quiet,
it's not because I'm distant
it's because I'm drowning
in how bad I need your face between my legs,
how you'd fuck me hard,
making me your good girl
until I'm trembling and soaked.
I could never tell you
how easy it would be
to let you have me.
How much I want to.
How much I already do,
even if it's only in my head.
I can't.
Because if I open that door,
there's no turning back.
And I don't know if you'd catch me
or break me.
So I smile.
I laugh.
I act like I'm not dripping wet
every time you say my name
But just know
I could never tell you.

Finally, he parked on Belle Isle, the water glinting under the moonlight. The air smelled of river, thick and electric. He tapped her thigh to get her attention, slightly gazing over to see what she was writing. Nia quickly shielded her notepad and climbed out the car.

They sat on the hood of his car, the city skyline stretching across the distance. Darius handed her a bottle of water, and their fingers brushed. That small touch was enough to unravel her composure.

"You ever feel like this city owns you?" he asked quietly.

She glanced at him. His hazel eyes reflected the skyline, softer than she'd ever seen. "Sometimes," she admitted. "Like no matter how hard I run, it'll find a way to pull me back."

He nodded. "That's how it is with me. With being D. But with you..." He exhaled, brushing his hand along her thigh, slow and deliberate. "What were you writing, Nia?" Nia slowly turned her head to try and cool herself off from the heat radiating between the two of them. She replied, "Huh?" Nia heard his question, and she saw him eyeing her notepad, so she passed it to him and held her breath as he started reading it. He finished it and said, "I'm glad you told me because with you, I get to breathe and just be me." Her pulse pounded. She turned, their faces inches apart. His thumb traced her cheek, and before she could speak, his mouth was on hers.

This kiss was different. Hotter, hungrier, pulling every ounce of air from her lungs. His hand slid to the small of her back, drawing her flush against him. She curled her fingers into his shirt, holding on like the world beneath them had tilted.

The heat spiraled—his lips trailing to her jaw, down to the curve of her neck. Her soft gasp escaped before she could stop it, and his low groan vibrated against her skin.

Her body screamed to give in, to let the night swallow them whole. But some small piece of her clung to control. She pulled back, chest heaving, eyes wide. "Darius..." Her whisper was half plea, half warning.

He rested his forehead against hers, breath ragged. "Say the word, Nia. And I'll stop." The restraint in his voice—the way he was holding back—made her want him even more.

She touched his cheek, letting her thumb trace his jawline. "Not yet," she whispered.

His lips curved into the faintest smile, though his eyes burned. "You're killing me."

"Good," she teased softly, though her voice trembled. They sat there cuddled up under the city lights, the fire between them burning hotter with every second of silence. Neither moved to end it. The wanting was its own kind of intimacy.

And when she finally slid off the hood, his hand caught hers, squeezing once before letting go, like a promise that this wasn't finished. Because it wasn't.

# SIX

# Surrender

In the following days, Darius continued to make time for Nia. Whether it was picking her up or running errands with her, just to be near her was the goal. Today they spent the day together at Summerset Collection. Anything she even stared at too long, Darius went behind and purchased. Nia wasn't use someone going above and beyond for her. After a day of shopping at eating at J. Alexanders, they decided to call it a night. The air between them was already beyond suffocating before the door even closed.

Nia barely had time to drop her bags before Darius pressed her against the wall, his lips claiming hers with a hunger that had been simmering for weeks.

The kiss was rough, desperate, but threaded with something else, something that made her chest ache, even as heat surged through her veins.

Her hands slid up his chest, feeling the hard planes of muscle beneath his shirt.

She moaned when his fingers tangled in the back of her hair, pulling her closer until he felt every inch of her pressed against him.

"Tell me to stop," he murmured against her lips, his breath hot, his grip firm at her waist.

She shook her head, voice a whisper. "Don't you dare."

That was all he needed. He lifted her effortlessly, carrying her through the apartment.

He stopped at the kitchen counter and gently placed her down.

He opened her legs and placed her feet on the kitchen island. He removed her dress and to his surprise, she was bare underneath.

As he stood in between her legs, he kissed and caressed every part of her.

She motioned for him to remove his clothes, and he silently agreed. Her eyes ballooned at the package being unsheathed.

The veins and the head of his dick was beautiful.

She wanted to trace her tongue along every intricate part. Nia's mouth watered as she took in the sight of his tatted, honey-brown, chiseled chest, his abs, his arms, his everything turned her on.

The way his body moved against hers was pure control, but the way his mouth explored her skin was worship—slow kisses along her throat, teeth grazing her collarbone, a trail of heat that left her gasping.

"Give it to me," she whispered, not being able to control her desire. He entered her in one quick thrust, meeting her demand.

They both stilled instantly as she adjusted to his girth, his pulsing dick already feeling like home to her.

Darius had to will himself to not move too quickly because Nia was soaking wet.

Nia held her body up on her hands and slid up and down his dick.

Their bodies collided again and again, not caring about grace, only need. "Nia baby, you feel so good."

"D, don't stop, please don't stop."

He stopped, stilling inside her.

Her legs instinctively wrapped around his waist. He carried her to the room, when he finally laid her on the bed, he paused, hovering above her.

His hazel eyes burned, softer than she'd ever seen them.

He entered her again, and she cried out in passion.

"D! Harder! Ooh yes, right there, baby."

He flipped her over and roughly slapped her ass while giving her deep backshots.

"What did you call me, baby?"

"Hmm?"

"Say my name, baby."

"D."

Smack.

"Umm" she moaned, trying hard to mask her arousal at him spanking her while digging in her guts.

His movements were poetic, rough but gentle, slow but deliberate, deep, but exhilarating.

"Say. My. Name."

"Umm . Ooo. D. Yess D."

Smack.

Smack.

He fucked her deep, moving in circles, learning and memorizing every crevice.

"Let's try that again. What's my name, baby?" he said, as he continued to swirl his dick inside her like a rollercoaster.

"D! Oh my God, D!"

"No, baby, that's not it."

"Baby, you're so deep," she tried putting her hand behind her to relieve the pressure, but he grabbed it, holding it in place while slowly dragging his dick up and down her pussy, making her whimper and beg for him to put it back in.

He shifted and began eating her from behind.

"Damn, Nia you're shaking, baby, and you're so wet."

Darius swirled his tongue around and ate her like a gourmet meal.

Darius growled into her center, "This pussy is mine."

She whimpered.

He sucked on her clit, making her inhale. "Is it mine, baby?"

"Yes! Yes, right there, King."

He continued to edge her, just waiting for her to say his name so he could give her what she wanted.

The pressure was killing Nia. She needed Darius to let her cum. She decided to play his game.

She turned over, licked her lips and summoned his dick.

His dick jumped in excitement. She laid on the bed with her head dangling and popped his dick in her mouth.

She deep throated him while hanging upside down, he fucked her throat while trying not to topple over from the euphoric feeling and the sight of her playing in her pussy.

She licked and sucked on his veins then asked him, "Is this my dick, King?"

Darius was done playing this game and was ready to get back inside Nia's warm gushy pussy.

Nia knew he couldn't last much longer after she vacuum sealed her mouth around his dick and slowly swirled her tongue around his veiny shaft. She removed his dick from her mouth just as he pulled back.

Darius's dick was throbbing, so he grabbed her legs, turning her back around so he could dive back in. "Nia, I'm yours and your mine and this pussy is definitely mine. Tell me, baby, are you mine? Mind, Body, and Spirit?"

Nia couldn't think straight because she was on the brink of release.

"Nia, is your mind going to daydream of me. Is your body going to yearn for me? Is your spirit going to desire me?"

"Yessss Darius, Baby! Yes, KIII-NNN-GGG!"

The release washed over them both. A dam breaking, giving them both everything they never knew they needed.

"I don't know what you're doing to me, Nia," he said, voice low, almost reverent. Her hand cupped his cheek, thumb brushing his jaw and she said, "Loving you."

The night continued to unravel in waves—kisses that deepened until she couldn't breathe, his hands exploring every inch of her, touches that left her trembling and arching beneath him. He moved with a mix of power and tenderness, taking his time, pulling sounds from her she didn't know she could make.

Every whispered "Darius" from her lips drove him harder, deeper, like her saying his real name stripped away every wall he'd built as D.

By the time they finally collapsed together, tangled in the sheets and drenched in sweat, the world outside didn't exist. It was just them, the thrum of their hearts beating in sync, the city humming faintly beyond the walls was no more.

Soft gray light had been filtering through the blinds for hours when Nia stirred. Her body ached in the best way, every nerve still buzzing. She turned her head and found Darius lying on his back beside her, one arm tucked under his head, the other draped across her waist like he had no plans of letting her go. She traced his tattoos down his arm, watching his softened features like he was at peace. His lips curved faintly, even in sleep.

For a moment, she just watched him. The street knew him as D, all sharp edges and danger. But here, in her bed, he was just Darius—unguarded, beautiful, hers.

She leaned in, brushing a kiss against his shoulder. He stirred, hazel eyes cracking open, a slow smile tugging at his mouth.

"Morning, Gorgeous," His voice was low, raspy.

"Morning," she whispered back.

He tightened his arm around her, pulling her on top of him. "You're dangerous, you know that?"

She raised a brow. "Me?"

"Yeah," he said, sliding his hand down the curve of her back. "You got me wanting more. And I don't usually let myself want."

Before she could answer, he flipped her beneath him, his mouth finding hers again, slower this time, but no less intense. The kiss deepened, hands exploring lazily, as if the night hadn't been enough.

She laughed breathlessly against his lips. "You don't ever get tired?"

He grinned, teeth grazing her bottom lip. "Of you? Of this?" he replied, rubbing slow circles on her clit. "Never!"

The sheets tangled again, the morning stretching into another haze of kisses and soft moans, their hunger reigniting like the night had never ended.

And when they finally lay wrapped in each other again, her head on his chest, his hand drawing circles on her hip, Nia knew this was more than just fire.

This was the kind of heat that burned its way into the soul.

# SEVEN

# Wrapped in You

The second time Nia woke, the room was still wrapped in light, her body tangled between sheets and him, her skin humming with the ghost of Darius's touch. He'd worn her out, and yet, he hadn't let go; his arm heavy across her waist, his face buried in her neck. She drifted back to sleep in that cocoon, comforted by the steady rhythm of his breathing.

The third time she woke, full sun seeped brightly through the blinds, painting thin golden lines across the wall. She blinked slowly, the memory of the previous night and morning sessions washing over her in waves—his hands, his voice, the way he'd whispered her name like it meant something only to him.

Her lips curved before she could stop herself. She turned carefully in his arms, expecting him to still be asleep.

But he wasn't.

Hazel eyes watched her, half-lidded, warm and unguarded. His mouth tilted into the faintest smile.

"Afternoon," he murmured, voice rough, still heavy with sleep.

She shifted against him, acutely aware of his body pressed to hers. "How long you been awake?"

"Long enough to know you snore a little," he teased.

Her eyes widened. "I do not."

"Just a little," he said, his smirk widening. "It's cute."

She groaned and buried her face in his chest, which only made him laugh—low, husky, the kind of laugh that vibrated through her ribs.

For a while, they stayed that way. His hand traced idle patterns along her back, her fingers playing with the chain around his neck. Silence settled over them, but it wasn't awkward. It was soft, comfortable, the kind of silence that spoke louder than words.

Finally, she tilted her head to look up at him. "You ever let anyone see you like this?"

"Like what?"

She gestured at the bed, at the soft look in his eyes, at the way his arm held her like he had no plans of letting go.

He was quiet for a moment, his gaze steady on hers. "No. Not like this."

The weight of his honesty pressed against her chest. She reached up, brushing her thumb along his jawline, feeling the faint stubble beneath her fingers.

"You don't ever have to be D with me," she whispered.

His hand slid down her hip, gripping her gently. "That's the problem, Nia. With you, I can't be D even if I tried."

Her heart clenched at his words. She leaned up and kissed him—soft at first, then deeper when he responded, his hand sliding into her hair, tilting her head back. The kiss grew lazy and sweet, the kind that lingered, their lips brushing again and again like neither wanted to break away.

When he rolled her onto her back, his body covering hers, she didn't resist. His touch was different this time—slower, more deliberate. His mouth moved down her neck, across her collarbone, every kiss a quiet promise. She sighed his name, her fingers curling against his skin, and his groan vibrated against her chest.

"Babe, we have to get up. We need to eat!"

"Nia, I'm about to get all the nourishment I need. Open up!"

Darius devoured her and they made love again, not with the urgency of before but with tenderness, savoring every gasp, every moan, every whispered name. He moved like he wanted to memorize her body, and she gave herself over to him completely, holding nothing back.

Afterward, they showered together, slick with water, their bodies pressed close. Nia's head rested on his chest.

He leaned down and kissed her again. This one was soft, lingering, carrying every unspoken thing she couldn't put into words.

When she finally pulled back, he tucked a strand of hair behind her ear. "Nia. I'm all in."

Her chest swelled, and she whispered the only truth she had in that moment. "Me too."

They stayed in their world, wrapped up in each other, laughing between kisses, stealing moments of sweetness between the fire that kept sparking every time they touched. The world outside could wait. Because for now, here, wrapped in each other, they had carved out something fragile and beautiful. Something that felt dangerously close to love.

# EIGHT

# A World of Our Own

The world outside kept moving, but for Nia and Darius, time slowed.

Days melted into nights, and nights blurred into mornings spent tangled in sheets, lips swollen from kisses, bodies aching in that sweet way only closeness could cause.

On Sunday, he drove her out past the edge of downtown, windows rolled down, music low. His hand rested on her thigh the whole way, thumb tracing circles on her skin.

"You trust me, right?" he asked, glancing at her.

She smirked. "Do I have a choice?"

"Always." He squeezed gently. "But I like that you choose me anyway."

They ended up at a small diner tucked off Gratiot, the kind of place with sticky tables and strong coffee. Darius ordered for them without asking, like he already knew what she wanted. And when the waitress set down the plates, he slid his eggs to her without hesitation.

"You don't even like eggs," she realized, brows raised.

He just shrugged. "But you do."

The simplicity of it—the quiet thoughtfulness—made her chest ache.

Later, they sprawled across her couch, takeout containers scattered on the table, a movie playing low in the background. Darius stretched out, his head in her lap, while she absent-mindedly massaged his scalp.

"You ever get tired of carrying all that weight?" she asked quietly.

His eyes flicked open, sharp at first, then softening. "Every damn day."

"Then put it down," she whispered. "At least when you're here."

He reached up, capturing her hand, pressing a kiss to her palm. "That's the thing, Nia. With you, I already do."

The heat between them came like it always did—sudden, consuming. She leaned down to kiss him, and he raised up only to summon her into his lap, their mouths crashing together. Clothes tugged loose, hands desperate, yet it wasn't just hunger. It was need, raw and undeniable.

When it was over, they lay there, her head against his chest, the rhythm of his heartbeat grounding her.

"You scare me," she admitted softly.

"Why?"

"Because I don't know how to want someone this much without losing myself."

He tilted her chin up, his gaze steady. "Then don't lose yourself. Just let me find you."

Her eyes stung, but she smiled anyway, kissing him again, slow and deep.

For the rest of the night, the city could've burned outside their window, and neither would've noticed. Because here, in their bubble, they weren't Nia and D.

They were just Nia and Darius. And that was enough.

# NINE

# Cracks in the Bubble

The week slid past like honey, slow and golden, every hour stretched thin between laughter, soft touches, and stolen kisses. Darius had a way of folding himself into Nia's world seamlessly. He cooked eggs badly, burning them twice before letting her take over. He carried her heavy catering trays without being asked, waiting in the driver's seat while she made her deliveries. At night, he sprawled across her couch, head in her lap, as she pretended to watch a movie while really just watching him.

It felt domestic. Too easy. Too sweet.

And that sweetness scared her. Because nothing in Detroit —nothing with a man like D—ever stayed untouched.

The first crack appeared at the corner store off Mack and Bewick.

They'd gone in for a Vernors and a bag of Better Made chips, her hand looped casually through his arm, the smell of fried chicken thick in the air. Two men outside fell silent when they saw him. Their stares lingered a little too long, heavy with something unspoken.

One dipped his chin. Respect. The other muttered something low. Not respect. Darius didn't stop walking, but his body shifted, subtle, his hand sliding across her back like he was guiding her out of danger.

Once they were in the car, she asked, "What was that about?"

"Nothing you need to worry about," he said, jaw tight. But the way his eyes flicked to the mirrors told her it was more than nothing.

Later, they lay tangled on the couch, the hum of the TV forgotten. Nia's head rested against his chest when his phone buzzed. Once, twice. Then again.

He snatched it up quickly, thumb sliding over the screen. The glow of his phone lighting up his tattoos, sharp against his skin.

"You gonna answer that?" she asked sleepily.

"Not right now." His tone was soft but clipped, his lips pressing into her hair like a distraction.

She let it go, but her chest tightened.

That night in bed, she traced one of the roses inked into his skin. "You ever think about walking away from all that?" she whispered.

He went still. Too still. Finally, his voice came, low and rough. "Every day. But it ain't that simple, Nia."

Her throat ached. She kissed him slowly, trying to soften what she knew she couldn't fix.

But when he rolled her beneath him, his mouth claiming hers, his hands gripping her hips like anchors, it wasn't just desire. It was fear.

They made love with urgency, his body pressing into hers like he needed to remind himself she was real, here, his. He whispered her name against her skin, his breath ragged, his movements raw, deep. Darius looked Nia in the eyes, hoping she could be his everything, and that he would someday be able to walk away from the streets. Their love making was poetic, they breathed each other, every thrust unlocking another chamber of her heart. Every lick tattooing his name on her body and marking her soul. He wrapped his hands around her neck, applying just enough pressure to make her combust. Her body shivered from the chill going down her back. Nia moaned his name repeatedly, worshipping his every touch. Darius made love to every inch of her body. Rotating between nibbling and kissing her softly on her ankles and then gliding his thick tongue over her white manicured toes. He sucked them one by one, before creeping back up to dive in headfirst. Nia gasped as he painted a sensual picture with his tongue. Sucking, biting, and licking while adding her taste to memory. Slowly adding fingers, curving them upward to find that spot to make her scream.

"That's it, squeeze my fingers, show me how bad you need it. Nia, look at me. Look at me, baby. Don't take your eyes off me."

As soon as their eyes locked, he felt her release.

Afterwards, he held her tighter than usual, his arms locked around her like chains.

"This kind of love scares me," she whispered into the dark.

He pulled back just enough to see her face. "Why?"

Her voice trembled, the truth spilling out before she could stop it. "I'm scared, Darius. Terrified of loving you so deep just to lose you to the streets. You're everything I never knew I needed, and it's killing me—wanting you this much, feeling you tear pieces of my soul away every time you touch me." So losing you would be me losing myself.

His jaw flexed, eyes burning into hers like gasoline on fire. "Then don't lose yourself," he rasped, voice low and dangerous. "But if you do, know this—I'll hunt you down, I'll drag you back, I'll find you every fucking time."

Her lips faltered into a smile, and she kissed him again, lingering, pouring every fear and every hope into the softness of that kiss.

The city pulsed outside their window, sirens in the

distance, bass rattling down the street, voices sharp with arguments that belonged to someone else's night.

But inside, in their bubble, it was just them.

Only now, Nia could feel it. The edges weren't as thick as before.

The world outside was pressing harder, knocking louder.

And she knew, sooner or later, it was going to break through.

# TEN

# The Other Side of Darius

I t started with a look.

They were leaving a small bar on the Eastside, the kind of spot where Nia felt out of place but went anyway because Darius wanted her there. The night air was heavy, thick with smoke and bass thumping from passing cars.

Two men leaned against the wall near the door, their eyes following Darius as he guided Nia to the car.

"D," one of them called, tone sharp. "Thought you said this was your block."

Darius's jaw flexed. He didn't stop walking, but his grip on Nia's hand tightened, almost painful.

"Ignore it," she whispered, tugging him toward the Charger.

But the voice followed. "Or maybe you too busy playing house with your lil' girlfriend to remember what side you on."

That did it.

Darius spun, his entire body shifting in an instant—no longer the man who kissed her softly in the mornings but the street D, all sharp edges and fury.

He strode toward them, shoving one against the wall with a force that made Nia flinch. His voice was low, lethal, his hand fisted in the man's shirt while the other hand was on his glock. "Say that again. I dare you."

The other one laughed nervously, trying to play it off. But Darius's eyes burned, his whole-body radiating danger, and for a moment, Nia swore the air itself went still.

"Darius!" Her voice cracked as she rushed forward, grabbing his arm. "Stop. Please."

It was the please that did it.

His chest rose and fell like he'd been sprinting. Slowly, he let the man go, stepping back, jaw still tight enough to crack.

The two men muttered something and disappeared into the night, quick to get out of range.

Darius stood there, fists clenched, shoulders taut.

Nia's heart pounded, fear and anger tangled in her chest. "What was that? You could've—" Her voice broke. She was hyperventilating. "I can't do this if that's who you are." she said breathlessly, holding her chest.

The words sliced deeper than she meant. His face twisted, wounded, but he didn't argue. He just opened the car door for her.

The ride back was silent, thick with everything unsaid.

When they reached her place, she slipped out without a word. He caught her wrist before she could close the door.

"Nia." His voice was low, raw. "I ain't asking you to understand everything about me. But understand this—you're the only thing in my life that feels real. Don't pull away from me now."

Her chest tightened, but she didn't back down. "I'm not pulling away because I don't care. I'm pulling away because I do. Because if you keep being D, if you keep choosing that life, it's gonna kill you—or drag me down with you. And I can't survive that."

His grip faltered. "It ain't that easy."

"It is." Her voice shook but held firmly. "You can't be

both. You can't be the man on the street and the man in my bed. You want me? Then you be Darius. Not D."

Silence stretched. The weight of her ultimatum hung between them, heavy as the night air.

Finally, he exhaled, shoulders slumping. "You're asking me to give up a part of me I've been my whole damn life."

She met his gaze, steady. "I'm asking you to choose the part that might let you have a future."

His jaw tightened, hazel eyes flashing with war between the life he knew and the woman he wanted.

Nia's voice softened, breaking. "I don't need a king of the block, Darius. I need you. The man who burns eggs just to make me laugh. The man who holds me like I'm the only thing keeping him breathing. That's who I'm falling for. That's who I want. That's who I love!"

Her words cracked something in him. He released her wrist, his hand trembling as it slid down to lace with hers instead.

"I don't know if I know how to just be him," he whispered, before getting out and rounding the car.

She got out and reached for him. "Then let me teach you," she said.

For a long moment, they stood in silence, his forehead pressed to hers, both caught in the gravity of the choice that lay between them.

Finally, he kissed her desperately, like vowing a promise he wasn't ready to say out loud.

And though fear still lingered in her chest, Nia kissed him back, hoping love could be stronger than the streets.

# ELEVEN

# The Call of the Streets

The next night, Darius found himself behind the wheel, cruising through the Eastside. The Charger hummed beneath him, familiar, grounding. Every block he passed whispered pieces of who he was, corners where deals went down, alleys where he'd fought to keep his name untarnished, walls tagged with respect he had bled to earn.

The streets called him like an old song, low and dangerous, reminding him of the man he used to be. The man he still was, in pieces.

His phone buzzed on the passenger seat. A name flashed across the screen: Tone. One of his boys. One of the last links to that world.

He let it ring once... twice... then answered.

"Yo, D. Where you at? We need you. Some cats from the West been sniffin' around. Disrespectful as hell. It's time we remind 'em who runs this."

Darius's knuckles tightened on the wheel. The words lit something deep in his chest, that old fire, the part of him that loved the rush, the power, the fear in another man's eyes when they realized who they were dealing with.

But then he saw Nia's face in his mind. Her trembling

voice. *You can't be both. You want me? Then you be Darius. Not D.*

His chest clenched.

"Nah," he said, voice low. "I'm out."

Silence on the other end, heavy with disbelief.

"What you mean you out? D, this you. Ain't no out."

"I said what I said." His tone cut sharp, final.

Tone cursed, then laughed bitterly. "Man, you lettin' that girl get in your head. Streets don't love you back, D. But we do. Don't forget where you came from."

Darius ended the call before the temptation could sink deeper. He tossed the phone into the back seat, chest tight, hands shaking as he pulled over and shut the engine off.

For a long time, he just sat there, staring at the dim streetlights flickering overhead.

The streets did love him, in their own way. They had shaped him, scarred him, made him the man everyone feared. But Nia's love—quiet, stubborn, unyielding—offered something the streets never could: peace.

He rubbed his face with both hands, then grabbed the wheel again, turning it hard. Instead of heading deeper into the blocks, he aimed the Charger toward Nia's apartment.

Nia wasn't expecting him. She was curled up on the couch, hair tied up, one of his hoodies snuggled against her frame. When the knock came, she hesitated, heart skipping, but something told her it was him. When she opened the door, Darius stood there, chest rising and falling like he'd just fought a war. And in a way, he had.

"Nia," he said, voice raw, stripped bare. "I walked away tonight. From them. From everything. I don't know if I know how to do this right. But I know I'd rather figure it out with you than lose you trying to be somebody I ain't anymore."

Her throat tightened. She stepped aside, and he walked in, filling her small living room with his size, his presence—but softer somehow, more human.

When she touched his arm, he caught her hand, bringing it to his lips. "I'm choosing you. Every time, I'm choosing you."

Her eyes burned as she whispered, "Then I'll keep choosing you too."

She kissed him softly, sporadically over his face, trailing to his neck while tugging to remove his clothes. She dropped to her knees and looked up at him with those eyes that told him everything her mouth couldn't say. Her mouth watered with seeing him remove his pants and boxers. Nia kissed the tip which seemed to blossom right before her. She devoured him, making him stumble, while watching him clench his eyes close, and biting those juicy lips she loved to suck on. Darius moaned out her name as she confirmed why she was his peace. He had never experienced a connection with anyone like he had with Nia. It wasn't just sex, she gave him purpose, saw a future in him, and secured every fear. He felt seen and that was hard as a black man in this world. Nia had him open, he looked down at her and when their eyes locked, she smirked and vacuum sealed her mouth while taking him further into her throat. He came instantly, holding her head in place as he poured all his love and admiration into her.

And when he kissed her, it wasn't the desperate hunger of the streets, but the steady fire of a man learning what it meant to be loved.

TWELVE

# Love and Consequences

Morning came softly, seeping through the blinds in golden stripes that cut across Nia's small apartment. She stirred first, her lashes fluttering as she blinked into the sunlight. The weight of his arm lay heavy around her waist, warm and protective, his fingers twitching slightly as if even in his dreams he couldn't let her go.

For a moment, she just watched him sleep. The hard edges of Darius smoothed in rest, his chest rising steadily beneath her cheek, his lips parted just slightly. She traced the tattoos on his chest with the tip of her nails, slowly, memorizing each curve of ink like it told a story only she would ever know.

He groaned low in his throat, voice thick with sleep. "You done starin' at me?"

She smiled. "Maybe."

"Don't stop." He cracked one eye open, hazel gaze glinting with a softness reserved only for her. "Ain't nobody ever looked at me like you do."

"Like what?" she whispered.

"Like I'm worth more than what the streets made me."

Her heart tightened, and before she could find words, he rolled her onto her back, hovering over her, his weight pressing her into the cushions. His mouth found hers, slow at first, then deeper, until she was arching against him, her hands clawing gently at his back.

"Darius..." she breathed as he kissed down her neck, over her collarbone, lower still. His name fell from her lips like prayer and surrender, tangled in gasps and whispered pleas.

They moved together as though the world beyond the four walls didn't exist—slow at first, then urgently, their bodies pulling tighter, closer, until it was impossible to tell where one ended and the other began.

When it was over, they lay tangled in sweat and warmth, her head pressed against his chest as his heartbeat thundered beneath her ear. He smoothed his palm up and down her back, steady, calming.

"Feels like the first time I can breathe," he murmured.

"Feels like home," she whispered back.

For a while, there was only silence. The peace of it sank into her bones, made her almost believe it could last.

But peace doesn't last in a city that never sleeps.

The first crack came that afternoon. Nia was in the kitchen when the sound split the air—a violent crash of shattering glass. She screamed, instinct dropping the plate in her hand as it broke across the counter.

A brick lay in the middle of her living room floor, surrounded by a spray of broken glass. Tied to it with rough twine was a folded scrap of paper.

Darius was on it in seconds, scooping up the brick like it weighed nothing. He yanked the note free, eyes scanning the jagged handwriting.

***D belongs to the streets. You can't save him.*** Nia froze in the doorway, arms crossed over herself as though she could shield her racing heart. "Oh my God..." His jaw locked, muscles coiled tight as he crushed the paper in his fist. "Motherfuckers think they can scare me?" His voice was low, dangerous. "They don't know who they playin' with." He started pacing, his body taut like a spring wound too tight. The raw power of his rage filled the small apartment, vibrating against the walls.

"Darius—"

"I gotta go handle this," he muttered, already moving toward the door. "Remind them who I am and that I ain't nobody to come for—"

"Stop!" Her voice cracked like a whip, halting him mid-step. He turned, chest heaving, eyes blazing. "This is what they want," she said, voice shaking but steady. "They want D to come back out. They want you to throw yourself back into their world. But you told me you were done. You told me you were choosing me."

His fists flexed at his sides, trembling from restraint. "You don't understand—"

"No, you don't understand," she cut in, tears streaking down her cheeks. "You can't fight this with fists and fury, or even that glock. You fight it by being Darius. By proving them wrong. That you're bigger than this."

For a moment, all he did was stare at her, breathing like a man at war with himself. His anger wanted violence. But her trembling voice held him like chains, pulling him back from the edge. Slowly, painfully, he unclenched his fists. His shoulders dropped. Crossing the room, he caught her face in his hands, rough palms trembling as he pressed his forehead to hers. "You don't know how hard this is," he whispered.

"I know," she said softly. "But I also know I can't love a man who's still married to the streets. I need Darius. Not D."

The note lay crumpled and broken on the floor between them, but in that moment, she felt his decision in the way he kissed her, deep and desperate, as if swearing to her in silence that he was hers and hers alone. But somewhere outside, she knew eyes were watching. The streets weren't done testing him.

# THIRTEEN

# Holding On

T he brick still lay on Nia's coffee table, sealed in the plastic bag Darius had shoved it into. After getting the window fixed and putting everything back into its respected places, she still hated it being there, hated the reminder that someone had tried to scare them, to scare her. But he refused to throw it out. It wasn't just a warning to him—it was proof. A line had been drawn, and someone was daring him to cross it. That night, though, neither of them gave the brick any more power than it already had. Instead, they gave themselves to each other.

Nia climbed into his lap on the couch without a word, curling against his chest like she was finding her safest place. He kissed the top of her head, breathing her in, his arm around her waist. Her voice broke the silence, soft as a sigh. "It feels like were being watched."

"We probably are." His tone was even, calm, but his eyes flicked to the window like radar.

Her head lifted at that. "And you're okay with that? Maybe we should go to your spot?"

He looked down at her, one corner of his mouth tugging into something between a smile and a warning. "Let 'em watch. We're safer here than my place but just know that I got you. Long as you know you're mine, and I protect what's mine."

Nia didn't know that Darius had sent a message to the fam and that they were good. He had them covered and better yet, he had a small detail on her to ensure it.

Her heart fluttered, but fear tangled with it. "That's what scares me," she whispered. He cupped her chin, tilting her face up. "You don't need to be scared. Not with me. I'll protect you with everything I got, and I'll make it back in one piece, that's a promise." The certainty in his voice was a weight and a comfort all at once. Before she could answer, he kissed her slow and sure, like he meant to remind her who he was with every press of his lips.

It started soft, then unraveled. Being this close, this intimate, always created this charge of wanting. Nia shifted in his lap, straddling him, her hands wrapped around him. His hands gripped her hips, pulling her closer, guiding her against him until her breath came faster, her body desperate for more.

"Darius..."

"I got you," he murmured against her throat, each word punctuated with a kiss. "Always."

His hoodie that she wore was now thrown across the room, his shirt soon after, clothes sliding to the floor like nothing mattered but skin on skin. He worshipped every inch of her, his hands mapping her curves, his mouth leaving trails of kisses that felt like sparks of fire across her body.

They moved slow, then faster, then slow, they made love in their own rhythm. Their gasps created a melodic soundtrack in the room. Darius drowned out every potential threat and worry. He applied pressure to her neck while sucking on her breast. Nia uno reversed his ass into the reverse cowgirl position. She wanted him to take her breath away and then slowly, deliberately readjust her pussy for only him. Nia wrote her name is cursive on his dick. Taking all he had to give. He fucked her back from the bottom then slowed when he noticed what she was doing. He thrusted up in her to snake his own name inside her. She couldn't believe the euphoric feelings that Darius could erupt from her, nor had she ever found a match that could beat her at her own sexcapade. He turned her around so they could stare in each other's eyes. The moment they locked, the orgasm catapulted them into an unexplainable sexual bliss.

When they collapsed together, nothing could be heard except the faint hum of the city sleeping. They sat in the moment, still tangled in sweat and soft caresses. Nia clung to him, burying her face in his neck. His heartbeat thundered beneath her cheek, steady and alive, anchoring her in the storm she knew was coming.

Later in bed laying quietly, she traced his tattoos with her fingertips. "You ever think about your future?"

He made a low sound in his throat. "Yeah."

"What do you see?"

"You." His answer was immediate. Rough. Certain. "You in my bed. You at my side. Don't matter where. Just you."

Her breath caught. "You mean that?"

He shifted, leaning on one elbow so he could look her in the eye. "I've never meant anything more. You're it for me, Nia. Don't ever doubt that."

Her eyes filled with tears, but she smiled through them, kissing him gently. "Okay." She signaled to do the secret handshake she'd created just for them, and he obliged with a smirk. They ended it, pointing at each other, kissing and saying "I choose you!"

They lay comfortably for hours, whispering, laughing softly, kissing in the glow of the moon filtering through the blinds. Holding each other like the world outside couldn't touch them.

But the world was always watching.

Around midnight, when Nia finally drifted into sleep

against him, Darius slipped from the bed. Barefoot, shirtless, he moved to the window. Something had tugged at him—an instinct sharpened by years of knowing when danger lurked.

A car crept past the building, headlights washing across the wall before pausing too long on the curb. His jaw clenched as he peered through the blinds. The car slowed, then finally kept moving.

His gut told him it wasn't nothing, but he shook it off.

Behind him in bed, Nia stirred, her sleepy voice soft. "Darius?"

He forced his voice low, steady. "Go back to sleep, baby."

When he crawled back into bed, she curled instinctively into him, her body trusting his, even when her mind didn't know why.

He wrapped his arms around her, holding her close, pressing a kiss into her hair. She sighed and settled, falling back into dreams.

But his eyes stayed open, locked on the ceiling. He'd chosen her. He'd chosen love.

Now the streets were daring him to prove it.

# FOURTEEN

# Peace Before the Storm

For two days, Darius gave Nia what she hadn't even known how to ask for: normal. They slept late, wrapped around each other, letting the sun crawl through the blinds before stirring. They shared showers that turned into more than just showers, water steaming up the bathroom, their laughter echoing off the tiles. He cooked breakfast once, burnt the bacon, undercooked the eggs, but the pride gleaming on his face made her kiss him thankfully anyway. The next morning, she cooked, and he leaned against the counter with his arms crossed, watching her move around the kitchen masterfully.

"You staring at me for a reason?" she teased, sliding a plate in front of him.

"Yeah," he said simply, his eyes locked on her. "Because I can."

His expression was soft, simple, and unguarded. Something she rarely saw from him. She tucked this memory away to hold, like a secret just for her.

That night, he drove her through the city in the Charger. Music low. Windows down. Detroit rolling by in neon and streetlights, half sleep but never too quiet.

Nia leaned against him, her head resting on his shoulder, fingers tracing patterns on his arm as the wind played with her hair. For once, she wasn't thinking about who might be watching. For once, she was just a girl in a car with her man, the whole city stretched out like it belonged to them.

"This feels almost too good to be real," she murmured. "It's real," he said, his hand sliding from the gearshift to her thigh. "All this! Me and you! It's as real as we want it to be." She tilted her face up, pressing a kiss to his jaw. "I want us to stay like this."

"We will," he said, glancing at her with a half-smile.

But the streets had other plans.

It happened fast. Too fast.

They were still laughing as he pulled up outside her building, her head tipped back as she teased him for getting turned around downtown. Him, the self-proclaimed "King of Detroit streets."

Then the night shattered.

**Pop. Pop-pop-pop.**

Gunfire cracked the air. The windshield spiderwebbed, glass exploding inward as bullets tore into the Charger.

Darius moved without thinking, instincts born from years of surviving. He simultaneously grabbed Nia and his glock, while yanking her into his body at an attempt to blanket her as she screamed, shards raining down like glittering knives.

The stench of burnt rubber filled the air as a dark car screeched past, tires howling. More shots spit fire into the night before the vehicle vanished down the block, taillights disappearing like predators slipping back into shadows.

The silence after was louder than the gunfire.

Nia's chest heaved under his, her fingers clawing at his shirt. He kept his body over hers until the world stopped ringing in his ears.

"You hit?" His voice was rough, frantic, as he pulled back

just enough to check her face, her arms, her legs. "Baby, talk to me—are you hit?"

"I—I don't think so," she stammered, her voice shaking, tears streaking her cheeks. "I'm okay, I'm okay—"

Relief crashed over him, but rage burned hotter beneath it. His jaw locked, eyes scanning the street, the shadows. "They came at you," he muttered, venom in his tone. "They knew you were with me." Where was the fuck was the fam that should've been on lookout? When he got out the bullet shattered car, he realized that the second vehicle was his fam that arrived in the nick of time. Nia slowly exited the vehicle going straight to Darius. Her hands gripped his face, forcing him to look at her. "Babe, are you ok? This is what I was afraid of! This is what I've been saying! They don't care who they hurt, Darius. They'll keep coming until—" She choked through sobs, "one of us dies or I let you go." The words barely made it out, getting stuck in her throat.

His stare cut into her, sharp and unshaken. "Listen to me. I meant what I said, I chose you. That don't change, not ever. They want D?" His voice dropped, deadly. "Then they'll find out real quick: D don't exist no more, but they must want him to come out to play."

Her eyes searched his, desperate and wet. "Don't let them drag you back. Be Darius—for me. For us."

For a heartbeat, the only sound was the drip of glass shards falling from the ruined frame of the car. He reached for her, his hand sliding to the back of her neck, his forehead pressed to hers. His lips brushed hers with a rough promise, a vow etched into the air between them.

"I will," he swore. "Whatever it takes, but first I have to handle this, or it won't ever stop."

Darius knew that Nia wouldn't understand that this isn't about him not leading, this was his opps trying to take over territory and with D not in place leading "The Fam," everyone saw his weakness and started making their own rules.

Nia closed her eyes, clinging to him like he was the only thing to keep her tethered, but she noticed the moment his mind was made up.

Snapping back into reality, in the distance, sirens wailed. The city watched. The streets whispered still, hungry, relentless.

And Darius knew: the storm wasn't coming. It was already here.

# FIFTEEN

# A Way Out

The Charger sat in the lot, its windows patched with duct tape and plastic, the bullet holes still raw in the metal. Every time Darius looked at it, his stomach knotted with rage. Not because they'd shot him. He'd taken bullets before. He could take a few more.

But they'd aimed at Nia.

That changed everything.

Two days after the drive-by, Darius sat in the back booth of a nearly empty diner, steam curling from a cup of coffee he hadn't touched. Across from him, his cousin Rico leaned in, his gold chain flashing in the dim light.

"You sure about this, D?" Rico's voice was low, like the walls might be listening. "You walk away now, they gon' smell blood in the water. You know how this game go."

Darius's jaw worked as he stared out the window. The streets outside were quiet, but his head was loud, buzzing with every move he'd made, every man he'd ever crossed.

"I ain't playin' this game no more, time ain't on my side" he said finally, his tone flat, final. "Ain't nothing out here but death and cages. I got somebody I can't risk neither of those for." Rico sat back, eyebrows raised. "You talkin' about that girl?" Darius turned, his stare sharp enough to slice. "That woman, My woman! And yeah. Nia. She's worth it." Rico studied him for a beat, then nodded slowly. "Then you gon' need a plan, cousin. A real one. No halfway shit." Darius tapped his knuckles against the table, the sound sharp, decisive. "I already got one. Just need to make it stick."

That night, he came home to Nia's apartment, exhaustion in his bones but resolve burning in his chest. She was curled up on the couch in leggings and his hoodie, reading the hottest new book in the city, Summertime *in the City*. She had finally started reading it after watching The Morning Collective on TikTok and making Darius take her around to all the local black owned shops to find it. She sat there, engulfed, with her curls falling over her face. The second she looked up, he felt that calm, that warmth. The thing that made every fight worth it.

"You okay?" she asked softly, setting the book aside.

He sank down beside her, dragging her into his lap, his arms wrapping around her waist. For a while, he just held her, his face buried in her neck, breathing her in like he needed her to remind him he was alive. "I'm done with it, Nia," he said finally, his voice muffled against her skin. "I'm done with the streets. With D. All of it. I'm plotting my way out—for good this time." She pulled back just enough to look at him, her eyes searching his. "You mean that?"

He nodded, his hands gently squeezing her. "I swear to you. I can't lose you. And I don't want this life to take from me no more. You're the only thing I want. I want to build with you, Nia."

Her eyes watered, a shaky smile tugging at her lips. "Then let me build it with you. I'm here, Darius. For the long run. You don't have to do this alone." Something shifted in his chest at those words, something he hadn't let himself feel in years. Hope and Love.

He kissed her slow, tender, not the fire that usually sparked between them but something deeper—like laying bricks for the foundation they both needed. When their lips parted, he whispered it into her hair, the words heavy with truth. "When this is all over... I want forever with you, I LOVE YOU." Her breath caught, her fingers curling in his shirt. "Forever," she echoed.

The city outside hummed, restless and watching, but in that moment, they carved out their own promise. A future. A way forward. And for the first time, Darius truly believed it might actually be possible.

# SIXTEEN

# Forever Begins Tonight

The night felt different. Quieter. Heavier. Like the city was holding its breath. Darius lay stretched out on Nia's bed, shirt off, tattoos dark against the low light of the lamp. Nia sat beside him, one knee tucked beneath her, her eyes roaming over him as if memorizing every line, every scar, every piece of him that had been claimed by the streets. "You sure you're ready to let it go? I want you to do this for you and to not have regrets" she asked softly, brushing her fingers over his chest. He caught her hand, pressing a kiss to her palm. "I've been ready. Just didn't have a reason strong enough to walk away." His eyes locked on hers, burning with quiet fire. "You're my reason now." Her breath hitched, emotions thick in her chest. "Then show me." What began as a kiss he planted on her palm slowly crept to kisses all over that deepened quickly, heat building between them like a vow only their bodies could make. Her hands slid up his arms, his strength melting into tenderness as he rolled her gently beneath him.

He took his time, worshipping her like she was his salvation. His lips traced every inch of her skin, reverent and hungry, until she was trembling under his touch. When he finally moved inside her, it wasn't the frantic need of survival or escape, it was steady, deep, anchoring. Every thrust, every gasp, every whispered "I love you" etched their commitment into something unbreakable. They moved together slow and sure, then faster, then slow again, losing themselves in the rhythm of devotion. The world outside fell away—no sirens, no gunshots, no enemies waiting in the dark. Just Nia and Darius, sealing their promise with fire and tenderness. When they collapsed together, slick with sweat and tangled in the sheets, she kissed the curve of his shoulder and whispered against his skin: "Forever." He turned his head, catching her lips in a soft kiss. "Forever," he echoed.

The next morning, Darius stood outside on the cracked pavement, the Charger gleaming despite its scars. Rico leaned against his own ride, smoking a blunt, watching him with curiosity.

"It was handled. You in the clear so you really gonna do this?" Rico asked, squinting against the smoke.

Darius nodded, his jaw set. "Yeah. Good looking, cuz. Streets don't own me no more. The Fam is yours if you want to lead. I'm done."

Rico studied him for a long moment before exhaling a slow stream of smoke. "Guess it's about time somebody made it out. You sure about puttin' all this weight on me, though?"

"You built for it," Darius said firmly. "I was just holdin' the crown until you was ready. You run it how you see fit. Me?" His gaze flicked up to the window where he knew Nia was watching. "I got a different kingdom to build."

Rico smirked, shaking his head. "Never thought I'd see the day. D, I mean Darius, settling down"

"Better believe it." Darius clasped his cousin's hand, pulling him in close. "Handle your business. Don't make me regret this."

"You won't," Rico said, though there was a shadow of doubt in his eyes—like he knew the streets never let go clean.

Later, Darius climbed the stairs back to Nia's place. She

met him at the door, barefoot, hair loose around her shoulders, eyes wide like she already knew what he'd done. "It's over," he said simply, pulling her into his arms. "Rico got it now. I'm out." Her relief broke into a smile, her arms tightening around him. "Then it's just us."

He kissed her deeply, like she was the only thing tethering him to this new world. "Just us," he murmured. "Forever starts now." And for the first time, he believed it wasn't just words. It was truth.

# SEVENTEEN

# Soft Places

The days after Darius handed everything to Rico felt lighter, freer, almost unreal. For the first time in years, he wasn't checking over his shoulder at every stoplight or reading shadows in every alley. He still noticed them, sure—a lifetime of instincts couldn't just vanish overnight. But when Nia's hand was in his, he forced himself to look forward instead of back. Nia blossomed in that peace. She laughed more. She cooked with music blasting through the apartment, dancing barefoot on the kitchen tiles, pulling him into spins until he pretended to groan about his sore knees. She painted her nails at the coffee table while he watched the game, then wiggled her toes in his lap until he gave in and rubbed her feet. Her softness was a world he'd never known he craved:candles lit for no reason, whispered prayers at night, long talks about nothing that somehow meant everything. He wanted them to get a new spot together, a place to make new memories just like he did with his car.

One morning, she woke before him and lay propped on her elbow, tracing the tattoos across his chest with lazy fingers. "You ever think about kids?" she asked quietly.

His eyes cracked open, a half-smile tugging at his lips.

"You tryin' to get me up early talkin' about kids or you trying to knock me up?"

"Knock you up?" Nia screamed. "Boy Bye!"

"But no, I'm serious," she quipped, her gaze tender but steady. He reached up, brushing a curl from her face. "With you? Yeah, I think about it. A little girl with your smile... or a boy runnin' around tryna act tough like me." She laughed softly, leaning down to kiss him. "Then we'll make that dream real someday." His chest swelled, the thought of someday settling in his bones like a promise.

# EIGHTEEN

# The Forever He Wanted

It was late, the city outside alive with its restless hum, neon lights shimmering like distant stars against the velvety darkness. But inside Darius's chest, another rhythm pulsed steady, determined, louder than car horns or the faint music drifting from passing cars. Tonight, he had made a decision that would forever alter the trajectory of his life.

He'd planned carefully, every detail chosen with her in mind. The black dress, silky and sculpted to her curves, was one he had imagined on her long before tonight and he just as vividly imagined sliding it from her skin by the night's end. Dinner near Greektown on the Detroit Riverwalk had left her cheeks flushed, her laughter spilling like honey over wine-stained lips. The atmosphere and views of the sunsetting on the Detroit River was breathtaking. After dinner, they walked the Riverwalk, mostly silent and enjoying each other's presence. "To be in a space where words weren't needed is a space where love can thrive." She thought about that quote that surmised her exact feelings now. Her fingers, small and sure, stayed laced with his as they climbed the stairs together, her presence grounding him, even as his heart thundered in his chest.

When he pushed open the door, the air inside seemed to sigh in welcome. Candles glowed in every corner, their flames swaying like conspirators, filling the room with golden warmth and shadows that promised intimacy. He had set them up earlier, pacing nervously, grinning at himself like some lovestruck fool who'd finally surrendered to his own heart.

Nia stopped short, her eyes widening, her lips parting just enough to let out a breathless whisper. "Darius...?"

He turned toward her, the weight of the little black box pressing against his thigh like destiny itself. His palms were damp, and though he had stared down enemies without flinching, tonight, his voice nearly trembled under the weight of his truth.

"I ain't good with words," he began, his thumb slowly brushing the soft skin of her hand. "But I know that every move I make, every choice I got left in me, I want tied to you. I walked away from the streets, from the noise, from the ghosts that tried to claim me... so I could walk into forever with you."

His eyes searched hers, raw and unshielded, as though offering her not just a promise but the most vulnerable parts of himself. The city could keep its chaos, its temptations, its darkness. He had already chosen his light.

And her name was Nia.

She reached for his face, with soft fingertips against his jaw, tracing his face. "Darius..." she whispered.

He swallowed hard, pulling the box from his pocket with hands that had once known only how to fight, to defend, to take. But tonight, those same hands shook with nervousness. He opened it slowly, revealing the diamond ring that seemed to shimmer brighter under the candlelight.

Nia's breath caught. The sparkle in her eyes had nothing to do with the diamonds but everything to do with the man kneeling before her.

"I ain't promising you perfect," he said, his voice low,

rough, but laced with a tenderness that nearly undid her. "But I promise you truth. I promise you loyalty. I promise to fight every day to deserve you, to love you in ways that heal, not hurt. I want to wake up to your laughter, fall asleep to your heartbeat, and spend every moment in between proving that the streets didn't get the last of me, YOU DID!"

Tears slipped down Nia's cheeks, but her smile was radiant, soft and big. She sank to her knees in front of him, cupping his face so he could see her, see every part of her soul in her eyes.

"YES, Darius," she whispered. "Yes. A thousand times, yes."

Her lips pressed to his, slow at first, then deeper, hungrier, as if love itself had been waiting years for this release. His hands slid around her waist, pulling her closer, feeling the warmth of her body melt into his. The ring box tumbled forgotten to the carpet, the promise already spoken and sealed between their mouths, their breaths, their hearts.

Around them, the candles flickered wildly, shadows dancing against the walls as if the room itself rejoiced in their union. The city outside continued to hum, but inside that small sanctuary, time bent, slowed, and finally surrendered, leaving only two souls tangled in love, choosing each other again and again.

# NINETEEN

# One Last Call

The ring glittered, joy spilling down her cheeks as she nodded, words lost to the rush of emotion. He slipped it onto her finger, her arms wrapping around his neck as they kissed passionately. But just as his world finally felt whole, his phone buzzed on the table.

Rico.

He ignored it, but it buzzed again. And again. Persistent. Nia pulled back, her forehead pressed to his. "You should get it." Reluctantly, he picked up. "What's good?"

Rico's voice was low, urgent. "Cuz... I need you. Just one last time." Darius froze, his gaze flicking to Nia, her soft smile still lingering, her ring catching the candlelight. The streets had let him go. But the question that still lingered was, was it done with him?

Forever looked different than she thought it would. It wasn't about diamonds or mansions or fairy-tale endings. It was Darius standing in the kitchen barefoot, tattoos on display, trying to flip pancakes and cussing when they landed half-burnt on the plate. It was him slipping his hoodie over her head when the night air got cool, even when he was left just in a T-shirt. It was the way his arms always found her in his sleep, pulling her against him like even his dreams needed her close.

Forever was simplicity, messy, and real.

On the night he proposed, Nia swore the whole city stopped just so she could have her special moment. Long enough for her to breathe it in and take a mental picture. She didn't need to see the ring to know her answer. Her heart had been saying yes to Darius from the very beginning—from the moment he pressed his forehead against hers and whispered that she was his.

Nia said yes because Darius wasn't just a man. He wasn't just the name people whispered with fear. He was hers. Her peace in chaos, her fire in cold, and her anchor in a world that tried too hard to pull her under. With him, she believed in forever. Nia could see their children laughing throughout the new home they built together. She never let a day go that she wasn't thankful for waking up to the sound of his heartbeat, and not the echo of gunshots. Nia believed in their love, even when the city was asleep and the whispers grew to screams that she couldn't have it all. Believing doesn't make it easy, but her faith was unmovable.

Because the truth is, the streets don't care about love. They don't pause for promises. They don't bow down.

She saw it in the way his jaw tightened when his phone buzzed. In the way his eyes darkened as he listened to Rico on the other end. He tried to hide it, tried to shield her like he always did, but Nia knew. She knew the way the past clawed at him, even as he stretched to reach for their future. Nia wanted to scream, to take the phone and throw it out the window, to demand the world leave them alone. But instead, she just held his hand tighter, letting her ring remind herself of his promise.

"When this is all over, I want forever with you."

She told herself that those words were carved into her for a reason and that they were stronger than fear.

Nia decided right then that she would fight beside him if she had to. Because loving Darius meant loving every scar, every shadow, every war he's ever had to fight. And if the streets wanted to test them, they'd soon find out that Nia had another side and she was ready to play.

## KISSED BY CHAOS
### By Shani Denise

In the heart of Detroit, love burns hotter than fire... and darker than sin.

Krystina has spent her whole life running from her secret — flames that leap from her hands when her emotions get too close to the edge. She's learned to hide her heat behind beauty, confidence, and walls no one can break.

Until Dre.

A streetwise dreamer with eyes that glow red when he looks too deep, Dre can hear every thought people try to hide — and Krystina's are the loudest of all. What starts as undeniable attraction turns into something dangerous, something fated... and something hunted.

As shadows stalk their streets and whispers call their names, fire meets mind, and love becomes the only weapon they have left. But in a city where power always has a price, Dre and Krystina will have to decide:

Will they control the chaos—

or be consumed by it?

---

🔥 A supernatural love story set in the real world, where passion is magic, secrets spark, and chaos has its own heartbeat.

# Let's Connect

Thank you for reading! If you enjoyed this book, please consider leaving a review on Goodreads, Amazon, or StoryGraph.

For merch, updates, and more about my work, visit my official site:

LinkedIn: Author Shani Denise
TikTok: @authorbydayreaderbynite
Facebook: @Author Shani Denise
Instagram/Threads: @authorbydayreaderbynite

Summertime in the City

Peaches wasn't looking for love when she came home to Detroit—she was chasing peace, hiding from heartbreak, and trying to find herself between block parties and steamy summer nights. But then Que rolled up in that candy-painted Impala, tattoos gleaming, eyes full of fire, and a past as complicated as hers.

He's the kind of man your mama warns you about—but your soul leans into.

She's the kind of woman he didn't see coming—but now can't let go.

As city heat rises, so do their feelings—slow kisses on porch steps, secret studio nights, and heart-to-hearts in the backseat. But when summer starts slipping away, so does the illusion that love will be enough. Life pulls them in opposite directions, testing whether this was a summer fling... or the start of forever.

One city. One summer. One unforgettable love.